Eileen Molver

Lindiwi Finds a Way

Illustrated by
Gary Rees

CHELSEA HOUSE PUBLISHERS
New York • Philadelphia

This edition published 1994 by
Chelsea House Publishers, a division of Main Line Book Co.,
300 Park Avenue South, New York, N.Y. 10010
by arrangement with Heinemann

© Eileen Molver 1992
First published by Heinemann International Literature and Textbooks in 1992

ISBN 0-7910-2915-8

Printed and bound in Great Britain by
Cox and Wyman Ltd, Reading, Berkshire

10 9 8 7 6 5 4 3 2 1

Contents

CHAPTER ONE

Lindiwi could hardly wait for the last lesson to end. It was a beautiful day. The sun was shining out of a clear blue sky and she was looking forward to playing a game of netball with her friends before going home. The school bell rang at last.

'Why are you standing around?' she called happily to the other girls. 'Where's the ball? Let's get started!'

The others looked at her. 'The ball's gone,' said Dorah. 'It's lost, or someone has taken it.'

'How can it be lost?' said Lindiwi crossly. 'It's always kept in teacher's cupboard.'

'Perhaps the boys are using it to play soccer,' said Thandi hopefully. Lindiwi ran to see if she could find the ball.

The boys were standing in an unhappy group. On the ground was a football. It was very old and had a tear in more than one place. Sadly it was almost flat.

'It has been patched so often that we cannot patch it any more,' said one of the boys. 'It's finished.'

'Have you seen our netball?' asked Lindiwi. The boys stared at her silently. They were only concerned about their own problem.

Fikele kicked at the old football angrily. It bumped slowly across the flat ground.

'We have nothing to play with,' he shouted. 'No ball, no goalposts, nothing. How can we practise football without a ball? Kicking a tin is not practice for someone who wants to join a real soccer team one day.'

Lindiwi felt sorry for him. She knew of his dream to be a famous player.

'If we could find our netball, you could borrow it,' she said softly.

'A netball!' he said in disgust. 'A netball is no use. It is not heavy enough. But I would borrow it,' he added quickly. 'It would be better than no ball at all.'

Lindiwi walked slowly back to the group of girls who were standing talking. Fikele walked with her.

'We have looked everywhere,' said Dorah. 'The ball is gone.'

Fikele shrugged his shoulders. 'We might as well go home,' he said.

'Wait!' said Lindiwi loudly. She was thinking hard. She was thinking so hard there were two little lines on her forehead. 'We need a netball and a soccer ball. How much money would that cost?'

'We have nothing to play with,' he shouted.

'A Jokari football costs more than fifty rand,' said Fikele quickly. He looked shy and rubbed his foot in the dust.

'I look at them sometimes in the window of the sports shop in town,' he said, still looking at the ground.

Dorah was shocked. 'Fifty rand!' she shrieked. 'For a ball? There are balls for sale in the bazaar that cost only two rand.'

'Those are children's toys,' said Fikele with his nose in the air. 'One good kick and it would burst – pow!' He clapped his hands sharply to show how the ball would burst. Some of the girls jumped in fright at the sound.

'Well, fifty rand or two rand,' said another girl, 'it doesn't matter. We have no money anyway.'

'We will get the money,' said Lindiwi firmly. 'Somehow we have to get the money.' She shook her fist in the air.

'Money for goalposts too?' said a boy eagerly. He did not know where Lindiwi was going to get the money. But if she did, they might as well get goalposts.

'And proper poles for netball,' added a girl timidly. They all stared in silence at the wooden poles, leaning over at an angle, which they had used for their netball games.

Until today they had been quite happy to use them. But now the idea of new equipment filled their heads. They felt they could not use the old broken things again.

Most of the boys had joined the discussion by now. Both boys and girls looked at Lindiwi eagerly. Her heart sank. What had she said? Where could she possibly get all that money?

'When do you think we will have them?' asked Dorah excitedly. 'By next week?'

'I don't know,' said Lindiwi. She really was in trouble now.

Then she straightened her shoulders and held her head high. 'By the end of term,' she said firmly. 'By the end of term we will have new sports equipment for the school. Football and netball,' she added, and then wished she had said nothing.

The children ran off to their homes, shouting in delight. Fikele kicked an imaginary ball as he ran.

Lindiwi walked slowly back to the school building and sat on the step. The cement was worn and crumbling. There was a hole at the side where a piece had broken away.

Then she started to think about the classrooms. There were not enough benches for all the children. Some of them had to sit on the floor. It was harder to work sitting on the floor. There were not enough books, or pencils, or slates. The teacher often had no chalk to write on the board.

Lindiwi had another thought. If we did have the money, surely those things are more important than netballs and goalposts. A map, she thought, with a longing look in her eyes. A map like the one she had seen in another school. The teacher could pull a cord and unroll it to show all the countries marked in different colours. The only map in her classroom was one taken from a calendar. It was so old that it was torn and curled up at the edges.

Lindiwi wished she had lots of money to pay for all the things the school needed. If she had money she would buy maps and books and chalk. She would buy netballs and soccer balls. She would buy, oh, everything!

She did not feel like going home straight away. She needed to be alone, to think. Lindiwi could always think better while she was doing something. She looked for a sharp stone and carefully scratched a hopscotch pattern on the hard ground. With her hands on her hips she hopped from one square to the next hoping an idea would jump into her mind.

You were silly to promise to find the money to buy the balls and goalposts, she scolded herself. Where will you get all that money? All the things

She hopped some more, thinking hard.

we want are very expensive.

She hopped some more, thinking hard. I wonder how expensive they will be, she asked herself. She wanted to have an amount of money in her mind to aim at.

'As if it makes any difference,' she muttered, her feet thumping on the ground.

She did not know where she could get any money at all. But if she found out how much the balls cost, it would be a start.

She decided to go into town the next day, to the sports shop Fikele had told them about. She would see for herself how much things cost. Then she would know how much money they would need.

As Lindiwi walked home, she remembered the look on the faces of her friends. They believed that Lindiwi would get the money. She stopped, and then she straightened her shoulders and walked on. She was determined that they would get the balls and other equipment they needed.

CHAPTER TWO

Lindiwi stared in the window of the sports shop, her nose pressed against the glass. She saw hockey sticks and tennis rackets. She saw lots of pairs of running shoes, blue and red and white and black. She saw cricket balls and tennis balls. There were roller skates and football boots. Fikele would love a pair of boots, she thought. But she knew that was silly. He only had one pair of shoes. How could he buy football boots?

There were no netballs in the window.

Lindiwi was nervous. She went inside the shop very shyly. It smelt of oil and new leather. There were shelves against the wall with lots of different kinds of ball sitting on them.

Lindiwi went closer. There was a Jokari football marked with the price fifty-five rand. That was what Fikele had said. A ball stamped with the words "Official Netball" was just a little cheaper. Lindiwi touched it with her finger. It was new and hard. She imagined how it would feel in her hands. If she had a ball like that, she could score lots of goals.

A man came out from behind the counter. He lifted the netball from the shelf and tossed it gently from one hand to the other.

Lindiwi stared in the window of the sports shop.

'A beautiful ball,' he said, 'and really cheap. Prices are going up soon. This is a good time to buy.'

'I do not have the money yet,' Lindiwi said shyly. 'I am finding out the price first for my school.'

Suddenly the man did not seem to be interested in her any more. He looked over her head at a new customer. He put the ball back on the shelf and walked to the counter.

A very tall, thin woman had come into the shop. She had lots of white hair piled up on top of her head. She wore round glasses with pink frames and a knitted woollen scarf. She had seen the man in the shop talking to Lindiwi.

'Do you play netball?' she asked Lindiwi. Her voice was kind. She did not speak as if she was talking to a small child.

Lindiwi said that she did, and then she told the woman about the lost ball.

'Has your school the money to buy a new one?' the old lady asked. Lindiwi sighed and shook her head. Then, surprisingly, the old lady began to smile.

She opened a big black bag which she had been carrying under her arm and looked into it. She took out a large, square piece of paper with printing on it and gave it to Lindiwi.

'That's how you can get the money,' she said.

Lindiwi stared at the paper. It had a lot of very small printing on it on both sides. She could not read all the words. The woman took it out of Lindiwi's hands and pointed at the words.

'It's an entry form for a singing competition, for choirs,' she said. 'Does your school have a choir? You do sing, don't you?'

'Yes, everybody sings,' said Lindiwi. She thought it was a silly question. All her friends sang, and her teacher, and her mother and aunt. And everyone she knew. They sang as they walked to school, or did the washing, or cooked their food. Singing was part of her life, like eating or sleeping.

'Good. Then you can enter the school choir,' said the tall thin woman. 'Your teacher will have to complete the entry form and sign it. She must send it to me.'

'But how can singing get us money to buy a netball?' asked Lindiwi. She was very puzzled. Perhaps the tall thin lady was mad.

'It is a competition for schools,' said the woman. 'It's held every year. I'm surprised you don't know about it. Each school enters a choir and the one that is judged the best will receive one thousand rand. They can buy anything they like for the school. Desks, chairs, sports equipment, anything.'

Lindiwi was so surprised that she dropped the piece of paper. She had to go down on her hands and knees to find it.

The lady closed her big black bag. 'You must show the form to your teacher. Get her to fill it in. Then she must send the form to me as soon as possible. That's important. The address is on the form. There's not much time left.'

She smiled at Lindiwi and went to the counter. The man began to show her boxes of tennis balls.

Lindiwi stood holding the piece of paper. She was so excited she could not move. One thousand rand! One thousand rand just for singing. If their school was the best.

We will be the best, Lindiwi said to herself. We will practise and practise until we are the best. One thousand rand! They could buy two netballs and two soccer balls, and soccer boots, and more benches, and – and – even a map that unrolled.

'Thank you,' she said to the tall thin lady as she walked to the door. 'Oh, thank you very much.'

Lindiwi ran home so quickly her feet did not seem to touch the ground. She held the piece of paper tightly in her hand all the way.

At home she had to help to prepare the evening meal. As she did so, she talked excitedly to her

'You must show the form to your teacher.'

mother and her aunt about the competition. She could not wait for the next day to tell the teacher.

'Don't get too excited,' her mother warned her. 'There must be lots of schools entering and hoping to win the prize. Some of them will be very good.'

'I don't believe it is true,' said her aunt crossly. 'Nobody would give away all that money just for singing. Let me see the paper.'

They sat at the table and looked at the entry form again. Lindiwi read it over and over, but there were some words she could not understand. They all agreed that "R1000" was printed in big letters on the paper.

'It may be true, then,' said her aunt. 'But it is a lot of money.'

'Miss Mabaso will be able to explain it tomorrow,' said Lindiwi.

Next morning she wakened early. She made breakfast, fetched the water and then ran all the way to school. She wanted to speak to Miss Mabaso first. She wanted to be sure about the competition before she told her friends.

She raced up the school steps and into the classroom. She did not feel the lumps of cement she stepped on with her bare feet. Miss Mabaso was already sitting at her desk.

'Quietly,' she said in a cross voice. 'You know

you are not allowed to rush in like that. Wait outside until I call everybody in, please.'

Lindiwi was out of breath from running. She was unable to speak. She waved the piece of paper at the teacher. Miss Mabaso stared at her in surprise.

'Singing ... ' Lindiwi panted. 'School ... money! ... Prize for singing!'

Miss Mabaso put down her pen and folded her arms.

'I don't know what you are trying to say,' she said. 'Take some deep breaths and stop jumping up and down.' She liked Lindiwi, but Lindiwi was always in a hurry.

Lindiwi took two deep breaths and held her side. She had a pain from running so fast. She was still out of breath, so she handed the paper to Miss Mabaso.

Miss Mabaso took the piece of paper and put on her glasses. Lindiwi thought she was doing everything very slowly.

'What's this?' Miss Mabaso asked.

'Singing ...' panted Lindiwi again. 'Sing-ing com-pe-tition!'

Miss Mabaso took a long time to read the paper. She turned it over and read what was on the other side. Then she read the whole thing again. Lindiwi began to hop impatiently from one foot to the other. Miss Mabaso frowned at her. Lindiwi took some more deep breaths.

She could hear the voices of the other children who were arriving at school. A ray of sunlight came through the broken window. It lit up Miss Mabaso's face. She moved her chair back a little.

Why doesn't she say something? Lindiwi thought anxiously. Perhaps she thinks we are not good enough to sing in a competition.

'This is very interesting,' Miss Mabaso said slowly.

'One thousand rand,' whispered Lindiwi. 'Think of all the things we could buy with one thousand rand.'

Miss Mabaso's face relaxed and a faraway look came into her eyes. 'Books,' she said, closing her eyes dreamily. 'Extra reading books for the older children. Oh Lindiwi, we might even buy a second-hand sewing machine. The girls could all learn to sew.' She opened her eyes. She had a lovely smile on her face.

'Oh, yes,' said Lindiwi happily. 'And a netball. And a football for the boys.'

They sat and talked for a minute. They counted all the things the school needed. Then Miss Mabaso tapped her desk.

'First of all we must win the competition,' she said. 'It will not be easy. There will be lots of schools. They will all be trying to win. They have been practising for weeks.'

'We will win,' said Lindiwi. 'We must win!'

'We will try very hard,' said Miss Mabaso. 'We will try as hard as we can. Now, call the children in, Lindiwi, and we will talk about it.' She took off her glasses and polished them on her skirt. She looked as if she was thinking hard.

Lindiwi ran to the door and shouted, 'Come quickly, everybody. We're going to sing, and earn lots of money.'

CHAPTER THREE

The children pushed in. They were smiling and nodding at each other. They had seen Lindiwi talking to Miss Mabaso. They were sure Lindiwi had an idea. Lindiwi was always having ideas. They all remembered her promise to get money for the sports equipment. If anyone could do it, Lindiwi could.

Slowly and carefully Miss Mabaso read from the paper in her hand. The class listened to her. Then they watched and waited. Miss Mabaso saw that they did not understand. Fikele scratched his head. He was puzzled. They were all puzzled. All they understood was that there was to be a singing competition.

'I'll explain,' said Miss Mabaso. 'All the schools sing their songs. Three or four important people choose the best choir. They are called judges. If our school wins the competition we will get a prize of one thousand rand. Think what we can do with all that money.'

'Netballs!' Lindiwi could not wait to tell them. She was jumping up and down in her excitement. 'Footballs and goalposts!'

'Books!' said Miss Mabaso.

Everyone began to talk at once. Fikele's voice

Miss Mabaso read from the paper in her hand.

could be heard above the others. 'A Jokari ball,' he said. 'Lindiwi, we would be able to buy a Jokari ball.'

'Better than that,' said Lindiwi. 'A Dynamic Arwa!' She remembered the name of the most expensive football in the shop.

Fikele sank to the floor. He rocked backwards and forwards with a dreamy look on his face. 'A Dynamic!' he said, his voice full of amazement. 'I can't believe it.'

Miss Mabaso began to speak. The class was quiet, listening to every word.

'We must win the competition before we start to spend the prize money,' she said. 'We must not count our chickens before they're hatched. Now, who would like to sing in the choir?'

Every single hand went up.

'We must start practising today,' said Miss Mabaso. 'There's not much time left.'

'The lady said you must sign the form and post it immediately,' said Lindiwi anxiously.

'I will do it today,' said Miss Mabaso. 'We must do everything properly, in exactly the right way, or they may disqualify us.'

The children looked at each other. They did not know what that was, but it sounded very bad.

'If the form is not filled in correctly and posted

in time, they will not allow us to enter,' explained Miss Mabaso. 'We must also follow all the rules. It is important to read the rules carefully before we send the entry form.'

Fikele looked worried.

'Please read it very carefully,' he said. 'We don't want to lose the money before we've even won it. We won't be able to buy books.'

The class laughed. Even Miss Mabaso smiled. They all knew that Fikele was more interested in football than in books.

Miss Mabaso looked at the paper again.

'We have to sing three songs,' she said, reading from the paper. 'A religious song, a happy song and a traditional song. We must decide now, because we have to write the names of the songs on the form.'

Everyone had their favourite song. The children called out the names of songs. Miss Mabaso wrote the names on the chalkboard. Then everyone argued about which were the best ones.

At last they made their choice and Miss Mabaso printed the names carefully on the form.

'We need a soloist for one of the songs,' said Miss Mabaso. 'Someone who will sing the verses on their own. Someone with a good voice.'

The class was quiet. They all wanted to be the

soloist, but many of them were nervous. They did not like the idea of standing in front of a crowd of people and singing for the judges. Not on their own.

'Each of you will stand up and sing,' said Miss Mabaso. 'We will see who is the best.'

Some of the children were shy and sang in soft voices. They looked at the floor as they sang. Some didn't know all the words of the songs, but they all tried their best. After Dorah sang her song they all clapped.

'Dorah!' the class shouted. 'Dorah is the best.'

Lindiwi was disappointed. She would have liked to sing the verse on her own. Lindiwi's voice was sweet and clear, but she knew that Dorah was better. If she could not be the soloist, she was glad the class chose her friend Dorah. Also she would be too frightened to stand in front of strangers and sing. It was better for Dorah to do it. Dorah was not so shy.

Dorah looked down at the floor. She pulled nervously at her cotton dress with her fingers.

'I will do my best,' she said. 'I will sing as well as I can.'

They all went outside into the sunshine. They lined up in rows, with the tallest at the back and the smallest in front. Miss Mabaso raised her arm and then brought it down. The class began to sing.

Lindiwi was happy as she stood in the hot sun. She didn't notice the smell of petrol fumes or the roar of the traffic in the road outside. She opened her mouth and let her joy and happiness pour out in the song.

'Do you think we will win?' Fikele eagerly asked Miss Mabaso when they had finished singing.

'We need much more practice,' Miss Mabaso said, shaking her head and pushing her glasses back on her nose. 'We will practise every day. I will get a book and make sure we are singing the right words.'

'I'm sure we will win,' said Lindiwi happily. She looked proudly at the boys and girls around her. Then her heart sank.

Lindiwi had never looked at her friends closely before. They were just her friends. They were all the same. But now she looked at them as a judge might see them.

They all had shoes, but some of them did not wear them to school. That did not matter. They could all wear shoes on the day of the competition. But some of the girls were wearing black tunics. Others wore torn cotton dresses in different

The judges will not even want to listen to us, thought Lindiwi sadly.

colours. Some wore clothes that were too big or too small.

The judges will not even want to listen to us, thought Lindiwi sadly. They will say, 'Who are these ragged children, all dressed in different clothes? What kind of school sends a choir like this to sing in a competition?'

Lindiwi felt a lump in her throat. She knew she was going to cry. She blinked away her tears angrily.

'We will win,' she told herself fiercely. 'We will look like a real choir. I will find a way. I don't know how, but I will find a way.'

Lindiwi thought about the problem all day. After school she drew another hopscotch game to help her to think. After two days there were little hollows in the ground, where she had hopped so heavily.

She was not worried about the boys. All of them had a white shirt. Dark coloured trousers all looked the same. The boys all stood in the back row, so their trousers would not be seen. No, Lindiwi was worried about the girls' clothes. Their dresses were all different.

About half of the girls had black tunics. Lindiwi watched and listened to the girls carefully. The ones who had the best clothes did not always have the best singing voices.

Lindiwi thought some more. She knew there was only one thing to do.

All the girls wanted to sing, and she did not want to disappoint any of them. But the prize money came first. Lindiwi went to see Miss Mabaso.

'The singing is good,' she said, 'but the choir does not look like a choir.'

'I know,' agreed Miss Mabaso sadly. 'There is nothing we can do. The clothes most of the children are wearing are the only ones they have.'

Lindiwi looked stubbornly at Miss Mabaso.

'There is something we can do,' she said. 'Will you let me speak to them?'

'All right, you can speak to them,' said Miss Mabaso. 'But I will decide who is to sing,' she went on firmly. 'If they all want to enter the competition then they can.'

'Did the form say how many people must be in the choir?' Lindiwi asked.

'No,' said Miss Mabaso. 'It can be any number. But the more children there are, the better the choir will sound.'

She looked at Lindiwi. 'They all want to sing,' she warned. 'I cannot tell some children they are not in the choir because they do not have good clothes. That would not be fair. There is nothing we can do about it.'

'No,' said Lindiwi. 'But we can tell them and then they can decide.'

'All right,' said Miss Mabaso. 'We will accept their decision.'

◇

That morning when the children lined up to practise Lindiwi stood in front of them.

'We will not win the competition,' she said quietly but firmly.

Her friends groaned unhappily. 'Why not?' asked Dorah angrily. She had been practising her solo very hard.

'Our singing is good,' said Lindiwi, 'but look at us.'

They were silent. Each child looked sideways at the next person and then looked down at themselves. Only those who were dressed the best looked pleased.

'Some of us must make a sacrifice,' Lindiwi said, and her voice trembled. She had to force herself to speak.

'We cannot all sing in the choir,' she went on. 'We must choose only the very best.' She stopped for a moment and then went on in a rush.

'Those who are not chosen must lend their good clothes to the others. All the girls in the choir must wear the school tunics. Then the judges will look at us and say, "That looks like a choir". Then they will want to listen to our singing.'

Everyone started to talk at once. Lindiwi waited for them to stop.

Miss Mabaso stepped forward. 'I don't know how the judges will give their marks,' she said loudly, 'but I am sure there will be marks for appearance – how we all look. We don't want to lose any marks. But the decision must be yours.' She stepped back beside Lindiwi and folded her arms.

Thandi said, 'Lindiwi is right. We must look like a choir. If we win, the money will be used for all of us. If I am not chosen I will lend my school tunic to someone else.'

'Thank you, Thandi,' Lindiwi said gratefully.

Other girls put their hands up. 'I will too,' said one. 'Me too,' said another. 'Only the best will sing,' they all agreed.

The children sang again on their own. This time it was more serious. This was not to choose a soloist. This was to decide who would be in the choir and who would not.

The final choices were made. Some girls cried with disappointment, then bravely dried their eyes. Girls in the choir tried on the tunics of girls who were not in the choir. They all talked and helped each other.

To Lindiwi's delight Miss Mabaso picked her for the choir. She borrowed Thandi's tunic. Thandi had not wanted to be in the choir. She was very shy.

When the new choir lined up in their borrowed clothes, Lindiwi was pleased.

'Now we look right,' she said. 'If we sing as well as we look, we will win.'

'The competition is next Sunday,' said Miss Mabaso. 'Those who are borrowing clothes will take them home on Friday. On Saturday you must wash and iron them. We must look as smart as we can on Sunday. Those who are not singing will come and watch. You must cheer as loud as you can for the choir.'

The clothes were carefully taken off and returned to their owners until Friday.

The last week seemed to fly. The other school work was forgotten. This worried Miss Mabaso, but all the children wanted to do was practise their singing. Finally Miss Mabaso agreed. She knew that nobody was going to concentrate on arithmetic or history.

The class would be working on an arithmetic problem. Someone would begin to hum one of the songs very softly. Then another would join in, until the whole room was filled with a buzz of sound like a hive of bees.

Miss Mabaso would sigh and say, 'All right, class. Put down your pencils. We will go outside and practise.'

They sang in the school yard with the sun beating down on them. The sound of their voices drowned the noise of the traffic in the road. Their clothes stuck to their backs in the heat, but they sang their three songs again and again.

It rained one day and they sang inside the classroom. There was a pool of water below the broken window, but this did not stop them. Their voices rose to the corrugated iron roof. Startled gecko lizards looked at them with big round eyes and a spider ran up and down his web in the corner of the room.

They sang on their way to school, and they sang while they were walking home. Sometimes Lindiwi wondered if she sang in her sleep.

After practice on Wednesday Miss Mabaso was satisfied with the choir. On Thursday Lindiwi was worried. She thought that Dorah was unhappy.

She spoke to Dorah after school. 'Are you nervous?' she said.

Dorah began to cry. 'Oh, Lindiwi,' she said. 'My throat is so sore. It has been sore all week.'

'But Dorah,' said Lindiwi anxiously, 'you are our soloist, our best singer. You must not get sick now. You can get sick on Monday, after the competition.'

'I'm not trying to get sick,' wept poor Dorah. 'What can I do? If I can't sing at the competition, we will lose and everyone will blame me. And we will never be able to buy things for the school.' She was sobbing now.

'Don't worry,' said Lindiwi gently. 'I will go to the clinic and ask for medicine for sore throats.'

'Please go at once,' Dorah sobbed. 'I must get better.'

'Come with me,' said Lindiwi. 'Then Sister can look at your throat and see what is wrong. She will put a flat wooden stick on your tongue and look down your throat with a torch.'

Dorah began to cry again. 'I don't want a stick on my tongue and I don't want anyone looking down my throat,' she said. 'Perhaps I will have to have an operation. Perhaps Sister will not allow me to sing. I want to sing on Sunday.'

Lindiwi thought that Dorah should see the Sister. But Dorah was very stubborn. If she did not want to go, nothing would change her mind.

'Then I will go to the clinic and ask for the medicine,' Lindiwi said. But she was not sure that Sister would give it to her.

Lindiwi was worried. The choir was doing well. They sang their songs beautifully. But Dorah was very important. If she was sick, all their hard work would be wasted.

CHAPTER FIVE

The Sister at the clinic did not want to give Lindiwi medicine for Dorah. 'Tell Dorah to come and see me here. I want to examine her first,' she said in a serious voice.

'She has a sore throat,' said Lindiwi. 'It hardly hurts at all. Dorah just wants some medicine. She is singing a solo on Sunday. Our school is entering the Choir Competition.'

'I don't like it,' said Sister, shaking her head. 'I'll give you a bottle of medicine. But tell Dorah she must come and see me tomorrow if her throat is still sore. She must come.'

'Yes, I will tell her,' said Lindiwi, taking the bottle of medicine. 'Thank you, Sister.'

'Good luck,' said the Sister, smiling. 'I hope your school wins.'

Dorah began taking the medicine. Lindiwi watched her anxiously. Dorah hardly spoke, and at their practice her voice was not as strong as usual.

Miss Mabaso was cross. 'What is wrong with you, Dorah?' she said. 'You will have to do better than that on Sunday.'

Dorah hung her head. But she would not go to the clinic to see the Sister.

Should I tell Miss Mabaso that Dorah is sick?

Lindiwi thought. Perhaps someone else could take her place. But the competition was on Sunday. It was too late. The whole choir would be upset. It might spoil everyone's singing. She didn't know what to do for the best. Finally she decided to do nothing and hope everything would be all right.

On Saturday Lindiwi carefully washed and ironed her borrowed gym tunic. Then she went to see Dorah.

'Did you take the medicine this morning?' she said sternly.

'Yes,' said Dorah in a whisper. 'My throat still hurts. I have a headache as well, and I have to go to the shop for bread.'

'Go now, then,' said Lindiwi. 'I will be back soon.'

Lindiwi's heart bumped in her chest. Dorah must get better, she thought. She must be better by tomorrow.

Lindiwi ran home and asked her mother for some of the leaves from the lavender plant that grew in a pot on the window sill. She put the leaves in a cup and carefully poured boiling water over them.

She allowed it to sit for ten minutes. She took the leaves out and carried the cup of liquid to Dorah.

'Drink this,' she ordered Dorah.

'I don't want to,' Dorah started to cry. 'What is it?'

'It will help your headache,' said Lindiwi.

Dorah sipped from the cup. She said, 'I don't like it.'

Lindiwi took Dorah by the shoulders and shook her. 'Do you want to sing tomorrow or not?' she shouted.

'I want to sing,' said Dorah. She had never seen Lindiwi look so cross before.

'Then drink it!' yelled Lindiwi.

Dorah made a funny face and drank from the cup. After a while she said her headache was gone but her throat was still sore. 'Shall I take more medicine?' she asked.

'Let me see the bottle,' said Lindiwi, still angry with Dorah. The label on the bottle read 'One teaspoonful three times a day.'

'You can only take three teaspoonfuls a day,' said Lindiwi. 'You must wait until later.'

'If three teaspoonfuls will make me better, then perhaps six teaspoonfuls will make me better faster,' said Dorah hopefully.

Lindiwi sometimes helped at the clinic and the Sister had told her many things.

'Six teaspoonfuls will not make you better any

She held her head back and gargled for a long time.

quicker,' she explained. 'Six teaspoonfuls might make you more sick. It would be an overdose.'

'What is that?' said Dorah.

'The label on the bottle tells you the right dose of medicine to take. If you take more it is called an overdose. An overdose of some medicines can kill you.'

'I won't take an overdose then,' said Dorah firmly. 'But I wish the medicine would start to work. My throat is very sore.'

Lindiwi looked at Dorah. Her skin seemed to be dull and lifeless, but her eyes were very bright. Her skin felt very hot. She tried to think of something else for Dorah to try.

'You must gargle,' she said suddenly. Lindiwi mixed some salt with warm water. She showed Dorah how to gargle.

Dorah thought it was fun. She held her head back and gargled for a long time. Then she spat out the salty water.

Lindiwi and Dorah talked about the thousand rand. It seemed such a lot of money that they did not see how the school would ever spend it all.

When Lindiwi left Dorah to go home she had done everything that she could. Now she could only wait and see what the next day would bring.

CHAPTER SIX

The children met at the bus station at seven o'clock on Sunday morning. When they had all arrived, Lindiwi looked proudly at the group. Their faces gleamed with cleanliness and excitement. Their clothes were washed and neatly ironed. They looked like a real choir, Lindiwi thought.

Where was Dorah? Lindiwi saw her standing on her own. She went to her.

'Did you take the medicine this morning?' she asked.

'Yes,' said Dorah. Her voice sounded like a frog croaking. 'I can sing,' she went on in that strange, hoarse voice. 'I know I can.'

'But Dorah ... ' Lindiwi began, and then she stopped. She had to tell Miss Mabaso. But if she told and Miss Mabaso stopped Dorah from singing, Dorah would not be Lindiwi's friend any more.

Lindiwi did not know what to do. With a sad heart she knew that they had no chance of winning the competition now.

Miss Mabaso paid for the tickets. They all climbed into the bus and started off. They soon arrived in town. The competition was in the biggest church hall. They walked from the bus station and waited while Miss Mabaso went to find out when they were singing. Lindiwi was very worried. She watched Dorah carefully. Dorah gave her a sad little smile. Just one little solo, Lindiwi thought. If Dorah could sing those few verses, she did not have to join in the other two songs.

Miss Mabaso came running back. Her eyes were shining with excitement and her glasses were sitting on the end of her nose.

'We are singing at eleven o'clock,' she said, pushing at the glasses. 'It's eight o'clock. Let's sit in the hall and listen to the other choirs.'

There were hundreds of children from different schools. Some had musical instruments with them, like drums and bells. Two boys from one of the schools had metal triangles, which they tapped with a metal rod. They sounded nice, and Lindiwi was sad that her choir had no instruments. Did the judges give marks for the musical instruments? she wondered.

There was a break at half past nine. The members of all the choirs were given cold drinks. They were all very thirsty. Some children bought packets of chips and sweets. Everyone sat in their school groups in the grounds of the church hall.

Teachers gave some last advice to their choirs. There was a hum of conversation and, now and

Everyone sat in their school groups in the grounds of the church hall.

41

then, a choir would sing a few lines of a song over and over.

'I don't need to tell you anything more,' said Miss Mabaso, pushing up her glasses. You all know what to do. I want you to enjoy yourselves. We'll all have fun today.'

The church hall was a big square building made of brick. It stood in large grounds with green lawns and beds of red, blue and yellow flowers. There were big trees with wide branches that gave shade from the sun.

There were crowds of children in the grounds and cars and buses were still arriving. They were bringing more school choirs and also people who wanted to hear the choirs. The people from one car had a small table and three chairs which they placed under a tree. They brought out cups and saucers, a teapot and a flask of hot water. They had a big cake in a tin. They sat and drank their tea, as if they were in their own home. Lindiwi could not stop looking at them.

Teachers from some of the schools asked their pupils to collect all the empty chip packets and sweet papers and put them in a bin. Lindiwi thought it was a good idea and went to help. The grounds were beautiful. All the rubbish would make them look ugly.

When she was finished, she went to look for Dorah. Dorah was sitting on the ground. She was holding her cold drink. She had not drunk it. Dorah was looking very sick.

'Are you all right?' Lindiwi asked anxiously. She touched Dorah's arm. It was very hot and dry. Lindiwi felt Dorah's head.

'You have a fever,' Lindiwi said. She was very worried now. 'Dorah, you are very sick.'

'I can't sing,' sobbed Dorah. 'I'm sorry, Lindiwi. My head is very sore, and my throat hurts so much I can hardly speak.' She could only whisper now.

Miss Mabaso came to see what was wrong.

'Dorah is very sick,' said Lindiwi. 'She has a fever. She can't sing now. What can we do?'

Miss Mabaso felt Dorah's head and said, 'Oh dear! Sit down, Dorah. I will try to find a first aid attendant.'

'Please, Miss Mabaso. It is almost our turn to sing,' said Lindiwi. 'Who is going to sing the solo?' She felt like crying.

Miss Mabaso was worried about Dorah. 'I can't think,' she said, with her hand to her head. 'I don't know what we should do.'

She took Dorah's hand and led her to some shade under one of the trees. She helped her to lie

43

down and then put her coat over Dorah's shoulders.

For a moment Lindiwi thought she was going to be sick. She was so worried. She closed her eyes and took three deep breaths. She thought about the thousand rand.

She opened her eyes and ran after Miss Mabaso.

'I will do it,' she said. 'I will do the solo.' Her stomach was giving little frightened jumps. 'I know the words and the music. I'm not as good a singer as Dorah, but I will try.'

She went back to Dorah. 'Don't worry, Dorah,' she said. 'The choir will still have a chance.'

◇

A teacher from another school had brought a first aid attendant. 'Don't worry,' he said. 'We will look after her. You go into the hall and get ready to sing.'

A voice on the loudspeaker was calling the name of their school. 'Do your best, Lindiwi,' Miss Mabaso said quickly. 'You have a very good voice. Forget about the people watching and sing. Enjoy yourself. Everyone has come to hear us.'

The choir formed two lines and marched on to the platform. Although Miss Mabaso was very worried about Dorah, she smiled at the choir. She raised her arm and gave the signal for them to begin.

Lindiwi stood in Dorah's place. She felt she was dreaming. She had practised and practised. She did not need to think of the words.

She looked down from the platform. The hall was full of people. Some were standing at the back. The judges sat at a narrow table half-way down the hall. There were three of them. They had very serious faces, and they sat with lots of papers in front of them. The tall thin lady with white hair was one of them.

Lindiwi's solo was in the second song, the happy, dancing one. She felt all right. Her stomach had stopped jumping. It was nearly time. The first song was over.

Lindiwi took a step forward. When Miss Mabaso waved her arm, she opened her mouth and her voice soared to the roof. The song was going well. She was enjoying herself.

She sang of happy people, of friends meeting, of sunshine and laughter. Her body moved to the rhythm of the music. When she smiled the audience smiled with her. The choir joined in with the chorus. They seemed to feel Lindiwi's happiness. The song danced along better than it

The song danced along better than it had ever done before.

had ever done before. When Lindiwi's solo was over she stepped back into the choir. She felt wonderful. She could have gone on singing all day.

The choir started the traditional song. The words and music, which everyone knew, filled the hall. Many of the people in the audience started to tap their feet on the floor.

When they finished the song there was a storm of clapping and voices shouted, 'Encore! Encore!' Miss Mabaso looked around in surprise.

One of the judges stood up. He coughed loudly and said, 'There will be no encores. We would like to, but we do not have enough time.' He sat down and Miss Mabaso led the choir off the platform. Her glasses had slipped down her nose in the excitement.

Lindiwi followed Miss Mabaso back to where they had left Dorah. They could see that the first aid attendant was still with Dorah.

'You sang beautifully,' Dorah said, sounding even more like a frog.

'Not as well as you,' Lindiwi said. 'But I did my best. Miss Mabaso, what is encore?'

'They wanted us to sing some more songs,' said Miss Mabaso. 'They liked us.' Her glasses almost fell off her nose in her excitement. She pushed them back quickly. She could not stop smiling.

'We all wanted to hear more,' said the first aid attendant. 'Oh yes, Dorah seems to have 'flu. It often starts with a sore throat. She should feel better in a few days.'

'When will we hear the results?' Dorah whispered.

'The judges will give the results after they hear all the choirs,' said Miss Mabaso.

'It's a long time to wait,' said Lindiwi. 'But they have to hear all the choirs first.'

All afternoon school choirs sang one after the other. Lindiwi sat and listened to them. Some of them sang very well, but nobody shouted 'Encore' again. Perhaps that is because the judge said 'No encores', Lindiwi thought.

After two hours she started to move about in her seat. She was too excited to sit still. When a choir sang badly she would say, 'We're going to win.' Then another choir would sing well and she would whisper, 'They are better than we are.' At last she could sit no longer. She walked quietly from the hall and went to the small room where Dorah was lying. She had a cold damp cloth on her forehead to help her fever.

She sat up as Lindiwi came in. 'Did we win?' she croaked.

'Shhhh,' said Lindiwi, pushing her back gently.

'Don't try to talk. The competition is not over yet. We are all waiting.' She sat on the bed with her chin in her hand and sighed.

'I don't know if we will win,' she said. 'I have heard so much singing that my head is going round and round. I don't know if we were good or not.'

'They said encore,' Dorah said, and Lindiwi looked more cheerful.

'Yes, they did,' she agreed. 'But there are so many good choirs ... '

'I think we will win,' said Dorah, trying to smile at the same time. Lindiwi tried to smile back. But her stomach was turning over because she was nervous again.

Miss Mabaso came to see how Dorah was feeling. She looked nervous too.

'The last choir has finished,' she said. 'We must go back to the hall, Lindiwi.'

'Come and tell me as soon as you can,' said Dorah in her croaking voice. 'I won't get better until I know if we have won.'

Lindiwi and Miss Mabaso walked quickly back to the hall. Everyone was waiting. People sat talking quietly. Every now and then a girl would give a nervous laugh. Lindiwi sat and waited, holding her hands tightly together.

We worked so hard, she thought. We must win.

But she knew that the other schools had worked just as hard. They must be thinking the same thing.

At last the judges were ready. They had talked and talked for a long time. They had all spoken and the tall thin lady had written down what they said. Now they had decided the winner. The thin lady walked to the platform. She coughed and smoothed down her dress. Like magic the hall was silent. The children sat as quiet as mice. Everyone waited.

The thin lady looked at the papers in her hand. She coughed again and someone brought her a glass of water. She sipped some carefully and put her handkerchief to her mouth. She looked round the hall. Then she dropped her papers and had to pick them up again.

Lindiwi was sitting on the edge of her seat. Come *on*, she urged the lady silently.

The thin woman patted her lips with her handkerchief. She looked at her papers. They were all mixed up.

Lindiwi gave a low moan and Miss Mabaso looked at her half angrily, half with a laugh. Lindiwi put her head in her hands and looked at the floor. She saw a dark stain like a netball and she put her foot over it.

'As you know we normally only have one prize

each year,' said the thin lady in her soft, kind voice. 'The singing this year was so good we wanted to award prizes to every choir. We all want to congratulate ...' She read out the names of four schools. There was loud applause all round the hall. Lindiwi listened, almost holding her breath. Their school had not been mentioned. She rubbed at the stain with her shoe.

'However,' the thin lady went on, 'the judges all agree on the winner. The soloist was excellent. Her singing was happy and clear. The winner is Jabula School.'

Everyone began to jump and shout. Lindiwi slid down in her chair and tried to make herself as small as possible. Tears came to her eyes. They had lost. They had practised and practised. But it was for nothing. They had lost. Lindiwi could not look at the faces of her classmates. She had failed. Her singing was not good enough. She knew how disappointed they were.

The thin lady was trying to speak above all the noise. Everyone was still shouting and cheering. One of the other judges banged on the table. Lindiwi was not interested. They had lost. She did not want to listen to any more talk, and she did not want to see Jabula School going up to the platform to get the thousand rand.

Lindiwi could feel the tears in her eyes. She had wanted to win so much. For her friends and for Miss Mabaso. Then she heard the thin lady's voice. It seemed to come from far away.

'I said that there is normally only one winner,' she said. 'But for the first time in the history of the School Choir Competition we have decided to share the prize money. I said that Jabula School had the best choir. But there is another choir who sang almost as well. Everyone here enjoyed their singing very much. Some people even called for an encore. This is their first year in the competition and the judges are sure that they will be even stronger next year.'

Lindiwi rubbed with her foot at the stain on the floor. No netballs or footballs or boots. No sewing machine. No map that unrolled. She had promised she would find a way, and she had failed. She closed her ears to the voice on the platform.

Then the hall was filled for a second time with shouting and cheering. Fikele was whistling through his fingers. Miss Mabaso was smiling and pushing at her glasses with her finger. She did not know what to do with her hands. Thandi gave Lindiwi a sharp pinch on the arm. Lindiwi sat up and stared at Thandi in surprise.

'And so,' the thin lady was saying, 'each of these

schools will receive a cheque for five hundred rand. The prizes will be presented by the Deputy Minister for Education.'

There was some applause for the man in the dark suit who walked on to the platform.

'Now,' said the lady with the white hair, 'I want the two soloists to come up and receive the prize for their schools. Once again I want to say well done to the two choirs. We heard two choirs today who enjoyed singing for us.'

Thandi pushed Lindiwi hard. 'Go on!' she whispered loudly. 'IT'S US!'

Lindiwi could not believe it was true. She walked on shaking legs up to the platform with the soloist from Jabula School. They were each given a cheque, and then they stood not knowing what to do.

'And now,' said the thin lady with a smile, 'we will have an encore. I want both of the winning choirs to come to the platform and sing for us. Everybody can join in if they wish.'

Lindiwi stood with her classmates around her as the words of *Nkosi Sikelele e Afrika* echoed round the room. She looked down at the cheque in her hand. Five hundred rand! *Five hundred rand!* She thought they had lost. She was sure they had lost. She remembered Thandi shouting 'IT'S US!' She

They were each given a cheque.

54

started to smile. She had found a way after all. She could not wait to tell Dorah the news.

As Lindiwi sang the words of the song, her smile got bigger and bigger. She had never been happier in her whole life.

Questions

1 Is Lindiwi's school in a town or in the countryside? How do we know?

2 What do the boys want to buy? What do the girls want to buy? What does Miss Mabaso want for the school?

3 How does Lindiwi learn about the singing competition?

4 How many songs do the children have to sing? What kinds of song are they?

5 Name three things Miss Mabaso has to do when she fills in the entry form.

6 Where is the competition held?

7 What do the children have to do to look like a choir?

8 Why is Dorah not able to sing in the choir?

9 Before she announces the winner, the thin lady names four other schools. What does she say about them?

10 Why do the judges decide to share the prize money?

Activities

1 Take a partner. Each of you should make a list of the things you think your school needs. How many of the things you chose were the same? How

many were different?

2 Draw a map of your school. Draw in each of the buildings, the football pitch, where the girls play netball, all the places in the school grounds. Don't forget to write the names of the places on the map.

3 For the singing competition, the class had to choose some songs. What songs would your class choose? First go back to the story and find out what kinds of song they were. Then choose the songs you like best. Can you sing them?

Glossary

appearance (page 30) how someone looks

applause (page 51) clapping and cheering

bazaar (page 4) market

decide – decision (pages 8 and 50) making up your mind

determined (page 8) going to do something no matter how difficult it is

equipment (page 5) things needed in school or to play games

expensive (page 8) costing a lot of money

faraway (page 17) dreaming about something

gargle (page 38) wash the mouth and throat with a liquid, usually medicine

imaginary (page 5) does not really exist

mixed up (page 50) not in the proper order

puzzled (page 12) did not understand

ragged (page 26) with dirty, torn clothes

sacrifice (page 29) give up something to help others

startled (page 32) surprised

stubborn – stubbornly (page 33) doing only what you want to do

The Junior African Writers Series is designed to provide interesting and varied African stories both for pleasure and for study. There are five graded levels in the series.

Level 3 is for readers who have being studying English for five to six years. The content and language have been carefully controlled to increase fluency in reading.

Content The plots are linear in development and only the characters and information to the storyline are introduced. Chapters divide the stories into focused episodes and the illustrations help the reader to picture the scenes.

Language Reading is a learning experience and although the choice of words is carefully controlled, new words, important to the story, are also introduced. These are contextualised, recycled through the story and explained in the glossary. The sentences contain a maximum of three short clauses.

Glossary Difficult words which students may not know and which are not made clear in the text or illustrations have been listed alphabetically at the back of the book. The definitions refer to the way the word is used in the story and the page reference is for the word's first use.

Questions and **Activities** The questions give useful comprehension practice and ensure that the reader has followed and understood the story. The activities develop themes and ideas introduced and can be done as pairwork or groupwork in class, or as homework.

Resource Material Further resources are being developed to assist in the teaching of reading with JAWS titles.